HOT·SHOT HARRY

ROB CHILDS

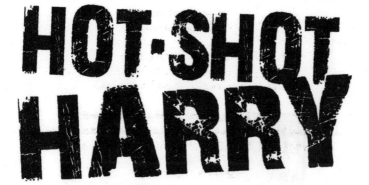

A & C Black • London

Contents

Chapter One

Five-a-Side

"Hot-shot!" yelled Harry.

Harry always shouted 'Hot Shot' when he scored a goal. That was why people called him Hot-Shot Harry.

Harry had just scored his second goal. It gave Gateway School a 2–0 lead in the final of the local Five-a-Side Festival.

Brad was the team's main defender. He ran towards Harry, and they slapped hands.

"Great goal, Hot-Shot!" cried Brad. "I bet we win the match now."

Just then the other side took a shot at goal.
But Gateway's goalie Charlotte dived and
grabbed the ball.

"Good save, Charlie!" cried Harry, giving
her a thumbs-up sign.

At half-time, their teacher told the players
not to relax.

"Remember, anything can happen in five-a-side soccer," Mrs Phillips said. "The game isn't over until the final whistle."

The second half of the match had only just started when the opposition scored.

The striker for other team sent the ball flashing past Charlotte. She didn't stand a chance.

Harry was furious.

"You're rubbish, guys!" he shouted. "Where was the marking?"

"Cool it, cousin," said Leela. She was the other striker. "It wasn't anybody's fault."

"Don't tell me to cool it!" snapped Harry. "I'm captain."

Leela gave a little shrug and turned away. She knew there was no point in trying to argue with Harry.

11

They didn't speak to each other for the rest of the game. Not even when Harry scored a third goal.

"Hot-shot!" he cried. "That's my hat trick."

The three goals made Harry the team's top scorer in the tournament. He had beaten Leela's total. She knew he wouldn't let her forget it.

The six members of the squad got their medals and Harry held up the silver trophy for the cameras.

"Well done, everyone," Mrs Phillips said. "Gateway School will now be in the County Finals next month."

"We seem to do better at five-a-side," said Brad. He was sitting on a bench in the boys' changing room and gazing at the medal in his hand. "We've lost too many matches this season playing eleven-a-side on a big pitch."

"Yeah," Harry agreed. "That's because we get rid of some of the dummies when we play with just five players."

Brad shrugged. "So which dummies are left in the five-a-side team?"

"My cousin, for a start," said Harry.

"Leela? She's good. I mean, she's dead fast," said Brad.

"Yeah, but it's not just speed you need, is it?" argued Harry. "You need a bit of strength and skill on the ball."

"I suppose so – but she can still score goals..."

Brad saw the look on Harry's face, and shut up. He didn't want to be put in the captain's list of dummies.

In the girls' room, Leela and Charlotte were also talking.

"He's cute, your cousin," said Charlotte with a grin as Leela came out of the showers, drying her long black hair.

"Harry?" Leela asked in surprise.

"Who else? How many other cousins you got?" asked Charlotte.

"I've got hundreds. And none of them are cute."

"Well, Harry can be – sometimes," Charlotte said.

"Really?" replied Leela. "Maybe you won't think he's so cute, Charlie, when I tell you he reckons all girls are dummies."

Chapter Two

In Goal

The boys were having a lunchtime
kick-about on the playing field.
"Watch this!" cried Oliver.

He was always looking for new ways
of celebrating a goal, but he was better at
football than gym.

He did a clumsy cartwheel across the
grass, followed by a bumpy forward roll.

"Ground's too hard," he muttered, rubbing
his shoulder.

Brad laughed. "That needs a bit more
practice, Ollie."

The girls were sitting on a grassy bank nearby.

"Just look at that lot," laughed Charlotte. "What a bunch of idiots!"

"Sure are," Leela agreed. "I'm almost glad they won't let us join in."

"You sound as if you want to," Charlotte said.

"No way," said Leela.

Then the ball came rolling towards them.

"Boot it back, Charlie," shouted Harry.

But Leela pounced on the ball and dribbled it to the goal.

"Come on, just give it back," Harry demanded, but Leela kept on running, with the ball under control.

Brad tried to tackle her, but Leela skipped past him.

Another member of the Fives squad, Ravi, was in goal, standing between the bags being used as posts.

"Come on, then," Ravi shouted to her. "Bet you can't beat me from there."

Leela's shot swerved past him and went between the bags.

"Goal!" she cried, and did a perfect cartwheel and forward roll. Leela was a member of the school gym club.

Harry pulled a face. "Huh! You ought to be on telly," he grunted.

"I will be one day," she told him with a grin. "Scoring at Wembley."

"No chance!" said Harry.

Ravi called across the field. "Hey! Charlie! You want to play in goal?"

Harry gave him a dirty look. "I told you. No girls."

"Why not?" Ravi argued. "She's the best keeper we've got."

"She's the only keeper we've got," Harry said. "You're no good."

"I'm better than you," Ravi snapped.

"You wish," said Harry.

"Yeah? Come on, then. Prove it!" Ravi yelled.

Leela liked seeing somebody else standing up to Harry.

"Yes, let's see how good you are in goal, Harry," she said. "If you dare."

Harry couldn't back down now.

"OK, then, I don't mind going in goal for a bit," he said. "But you two still can't play."

"That's all right," Leela smiled. "We'll just watch."

The two girls stood right behind the goal, knowing that would annoy Harry and might help to put him off.

"Clear off!" he told them.

"No," said Charlotte.

"Charlie wants to watch you in goal." Leela grinned. "She thinks you're cute."

Charlotte giggled. Harry glared at both of them.

"Keep your eyes on the game, not Charlie," Leela told Harry.

"Mark your man," Harry shouted at his defenders. "Ravi – you take Ollie. Brad, back him up."

Oliver was very hard to mark. He seemed to drift into spaces that no other players had noticed.

He found a space now. As the ball floated onto the goalmouth, Ollie timed his run perfectly. He reached the ball before Harry, kicking it past him and between the bags.

"Oops!" giggled Charlotte. "You missed that one, Harry."

"A bit slow off your line there," mocked Leela.

"Like to see you do any better," Harry snarled as he tramped past to collect the ball.

"Charlie would have saved it," Leela said.

Harry booted the ball away as hard as he could.

Harry was soon called into action once more. This time he made a fine save, diving onto the ball and stopping it.

"Good stop," said Charlotte.

But another goal soon wiped the smile off Harry's face. He got a hand to the ball, but he failed to stop it. The ball hit one of the bags and went in.

Harry lay on the grass, furious.

"Bad luck," said Charlotte.

Leela did not say anything. She didn't
need to. Ravi, however, couldn't resist.

"Do you still think you're better than me
in goal?" he grinned. "Or Charlie?"

Harry jumped up and lashed out with his
fists, taking Ravi by surprise. Then Ravi
knocked Harry down onto the ground.

"Fight! Fight!" went up the chant from the other boys, and a crowd gathered round to watch.

"Uh-oh," hissed Leela, taking Charlotte's arm. "Look, a teacher's coming. Let's go."

Ravi and Harry were still throwing punches as Leela dragged Charlotte away.

"Shame," said Charlotte. "I'd have liked to see who won."

Chapter Three

Injury Time

Harry and Ravi were banned from playing in the next eleven-a-side match. The team missed both boys. They also missed a lot of chances. Gateway lost the game.

"We were awful," Oliver groaned as the players left the field.

"Not my fault," Brad muttered. He was captain for the day.

As they sat on a bench outside the school building to take off their boots, Harry came over. He had been watching the game from the touchline.

"We deserved a draw," he said, pulling a face.

Oliver peeled a chunk of mud from between his studs and tossed it away. He had scored twice in the match, but was cross that he had not made it a hat-trick.

"Wish we got paid for scoring goals," he said.

"Yeah," Harry agreed. "I'd be rich!"

"Yeah, right," grunted Brad.

"Hey! I've just had a great idea!" cried Oliver, jumping up – and standing right in a puddle of water in his socks.

"What's that?" asked Harry.

"Getting paid for scoring! We could be sponsored for every goal."

Harry liked the sound of that. "Yeah, we could raise loads of money!"

"But the season's nearly over," said Brad. "It wouldn't be worth it."

"The Fives!" Harry exclaimed. "We could get people to sponsor us in the County Finals!"

Mrs Phillips thought it was a good idea, too, when the boys told the teacher of their plans the next day.

"What do you want to raise the money for?" she asked.

"We want to send it to that school in West Africa," Harry said. "The one we're twinned with."

"You mean Saint Francis School in Kenya," Mrs Phillips told him, with a smile.

"We could buy some sports stuff for the kids there to use," Harry went on. "Soccer kit, boots and footballs."

Brad and Ravi designed a sponsor form in art class that afternoon, and the other players made posters to tell people about the project.

"We want the whole school to back us," said Leela. "Everybody can take a form home and get sponsors."

"The more money we raise, the better," agreed Charlotte. "But we don't have much time."

The County Finals were only a fortnight away.

The players trained in the sports hall. Today Harry was on top form.

"Got my shooting boots on," he cried after scoring again.

"Shooting boots?" laughed Oliver. "You mean your scruffy old trainers!"

"They might be old, but they're deadly,"
Harry said with a grin. "I can't miss when
I'm wearing these things."

He was wrong.

In the next attack, Harry got past Brad but
Charlotte still stood in his way.

Harry did a little shimmy, hoping to
wrong-foot her, but Charlotte was not fooled.
She held her position, knowing Harry could
not try to dribble past her, as no-one else was
allowed into the goal area.

Harry was forced to shoot early, but she stuck out a foot and got the ball to safety.

Leela was the first to realise that Charlotte was hurt.

"What's up, Charlie? Are you OK?" Leela asked.

"It's my ankle," Charlotte groaned, taking off her right shoe so that she could rub the sore area. "I think I've twisted it."

Charlotte went off and Ravi took her place in goal. He started well enough by making a smart save, but then he let the ball slip through his grasp into the net.

"Try and get part of your body behind your hands," Mrs Phillips called to him. "That gives you another way to stop the ball."

"It's only a practice," Ravi said under his breath. "Doesn't matter if I let in one or two goals."

But by the time the session ended, Harry had scored another three goals.

"You're a rubbish goalie," he said to Ravi in the changing room. "Charlie's better than you on one leg."

"Huh!" Ravi retorted. "I wasn't trying, was I?"

"Course you were. You're just useless," said Harry.

"Cool it, you two," said Oliver, stepping between them. "It doesn't matter. Let's just hope Charlie's fit again soon."

At that moment, Mrs Phillips was looking at Charlotte's ankle.

"I think it will need to be strapped up for a while," she said.

"I'll be all right for the Fives, won't I?" Charlotte asked.

"You'll have to be," Leela told her. "None of the boys are any good in goal."

Chapter Four

County Cup

"It'll be awful if we don't score any goals," Brad remarked. "Loads of kids are helping to raise money."

"No worries," Harry said. He was sure he would score.

"If the worst came to the worst," said Oliver, grinning, "we could collect the money for each goal we let in!"

Even Harry was now worried about Charlotte's ankle injury. She was still limping around school and had taken no part in practice sessions.

"I'll be OK," she said again and again. "I don't need to kick the ball, anyway. I throw it most of the time."

At last Mrs Phillips decided Charlotte was just about well enough to play.

"At least people won't see the strapping on my leg," grinned Charlotte. "I'll be wearing my lucky red trousers."

Charlotte had worn the same pair of tracksuit trousers for the whole season.

The squad arrived at the city's main sports centre for the finals in high spirits. The eight teams had all brought lots of supporters and there were plenty of people to cheer.

"Come on, the Reds!" shouted Harry's dad as Harry led the side out into the arena. "Show them how good you are."

Secretly, Harry's dad hoped that Gateway were not going to be *that* good. He had agreed to pay two pounds for every goal that Harry scored and a pound for other scorers.

Gateway were in Group A, made up of four teams. After the first game, Harry's dad began to think the day might turn out to be pretty cheap. Gateway failed to score at all, losing 2–0 to Ashfield School.

The players couldn't believe how bad they had been.

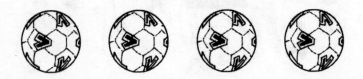

"We were rubbish!" groaned Oliver, who had missed the best chance of the game.

"If we don't win the next game, we'll be out," Brad moaned. He had scored an own goal.

At least Charlotte's ankle wasn't too bad, although it did still hurt a little.

"How does it feel?" asked Leela, while they watched another group game being played.

"OK," Charlotte lied.

Leela said nothing more. She knew that Charlotte would hide any pain for as long as possible.

It was soon Gateway's turn to play their second match. That started as badly as the first.

Even if Charlotte had been fully fit, she would not have been able to stop the ball going into her net after only a minute's play.

"Never mind, Gateway," called out Mrs Phillips. "Just get on with the game."

And the players got on with it. Leela drove the ball low into the bottom corner of the net, and danced a little jig of delight.

Then Harry's marker slipped. That gave Harry enough space to blast the ball past the keeper. Now Gateway led 2–1.

"Hot-shot!" Harry yelled then carried the ball back to the centre-spot himself. "Come on, guys! More goals mean more money."

Harry scored the next goal, too, shooting home from Oliver's pass to secure a 3–1 victory.

After the other two teams had played
their next match, Ashfield topped the group.
Gateway had one more game to play, against
Denton School.

"We'll qualify for the semis if we win or
draw," said Oliver, checking the tables on the
big display board.

"Yeah, but if Denton beat us, we're out,"
Ravi said.

Oliver gave a shrug. "Well, we'll just have to make sure we win."

"A draw will do," said Brad.

But Harry was not playing for a draw.

"We're going to win," he told his team. "And score as many goals as we can."

There were lots of goals. Neither side could hold onto a lead for long. At the final whistle, it was 3–3, and Oliver had scored a hat-trick.

"Told you it'd be a draw," grinned Ravi.

"Yeah, well, at least we scored a few," said Harry, although he was cross that he had not added any goals. His best effort had clanged against the metal crossbar, but it did not go in.

"Take a break now," Mrs Phillips told the players. "There's a short interval before the semi-finals."

"Who are we playing?" asked Oliver.

"A school from the city," said the teacher. "York Juniors. They won Group B."

Mrs Phillips took Charlotte to one side to check how she was.

"I'll be all right, Miss," Charlotte insisted. "I feel fine."

Leela guessed that her friend was not telling the truth.

"Keep it up, Charlie," she said when the teacher had moved away. "Do you want some ice?"

"An ice cream?" asked Charlotte hopefully.

"No, some ice to put on that ankle!" said Leela.

Chapter Five

Semi-Final

Harry gathered the Gateway squad
together. He wanted to have his own team
talk before Mrs Phillips came to take over.

"Right, guys, let's get ready," he said. "Dad saw this York lot win one of their games, and he says they play hard. Don't try anything fancy, Leela, or they will be after you."

"Then we'll get a few free kicks, won't we?" she replied.

"Depends on the ref," Harry said. "Anyway, we don't want these guys thinking they can walk all over us. We give as good as we get – OK?"

"OK!" echoed the other players as Mrs Phillips came over.

"Good luck, everyone," she said. "As long as you do your best, it doesn't matter about the result."

"Huh!" grunted Harry under his breath. "A win is the only result we want."

Harry's dad was right about York School. The very first time that Harry got the ball, a defender clattered into him from behind and left him lying on the floor.

Peeep!

Harry jumped to his feet when the whistle went, keen to take the free kick himself.

He kicked the ball low and hard, but the keeper threw himself to his right and turned the ball away to safety.

As Harry had warned, Leela came in for some rough treatment when she tried to run with the ball.

She was knocked down twice. The second time, the referee awarded another free kick.

York expected Harry to go for a goal, but he tricked them by slipping the ball into space on his right instead. Oliver was ready for it, and he steered the ball into the corner of the net with the side of his foot.

"Wicked, Ollie!" cried Harry, jumping onto his back.

But that was their only success of the first half. By half time, Gateway found themselves 2–1 down. York had scored twice in a minute and Brad was to blame for both goals.

"You dummy!" snapped Harry.

"Never mind, Bradley, these things happen," Mrs Phillips told him, but she replaced Brad with Ravi for the second half.

Ravi was on top form. Thanks to his defending, Charlotte only had to make a couple of saves, although one of them was brilliant. She dived low to her left to grab the ball, snuggling it to her chest so that it could not escape.

"Top stop, Charlie!" Harry shouted.

"To me, Charlie!" cried Leela as the goalie got back to her feet.

Charlie rolled the ball into Leela's path. Two York players tried to trip Leela as she sprinted forward, but her speed and balance fooled them. Glancing up, she saw that Harry had found space to her left.

Her pass was perfect. Harry did not even have to control the ball and he hit it firmly, past the York keeper.

"Hot-shot!" he bellowed at the top of his voice.

At full-time, the teams were still locked at 2–2.

"There will now be a shoot-out to decide which school goes through to the Final," called the referee. "Choose three players to take the penalties."

Mrs Phillips had already made her choice, Gateway's main scorers – Oliver, Leela and Harry.

"Do these goals count for the sponsor money?" asked Oliver.

"Course they do," Harry said firmly. "Goals are goals!"

Oliver took the first spot-kick, but he sent the ball high over the crossbar.

Harry glared at him. "Great!" he said nastily. "Thanks a bunch."

The first York kicker also missed with a wild shot, and then it was Leela's turn.

"Keep it low," hissed Harry as Leela walked by him, trying not to show how nervous she felt.

Her hands were shaking as she settled the ball on the penalty spot.

She met the keeper's eye on purpose, and flicked a glance towards the bottom corner of the goal, to his right.

The boy thought it was a trick and dived to his left, but it was a double bluff. The ball zipped into the other corner. Leela threw her arms up into the air in relief.

"One-nil to Gateway," called the referee.

Thirty seconds later it was one goal each. Charlotte had dived the wrong way too.

Harry showed no sign of nerves. He didn't have special tricks for penalties, like Leela's mind-games. He simply pretended that the goalie was not there. He always practised penalties without one and now he kicked the ball as hard as he could. The keeper jumped out of the way!

"Two–one to Gateway."

York took their last shot. It was a hard ball too, and Charlotte was not as sensible as the York keeper. She blocked the fierce shot with her right hand.

Gateway had won the semi-final!

Charlotte's cry of pain was lost in the crowd's cheers. Her team-mates all jumped on top of her.

It was only when she didn't get up that they realised she had been hurt. It wasn't her ankle this time, but her hand.

"I've bust my little finger," she wailed.

It was dislocated. A first-aid attendant put the finger back into position, but it was still very sore.

"No Final for you, I'm afraid," Mrs Phillips told her. "Somebody else will have to go in goal."

"Don't look at me," said Ravi.

"I'll do it," Harry said, to everyone's surprise. "Captain's duty."

Chapter Six

The Final

"They say all goalies are crazy," Leela told Charlotte. "And Harry sure is crazy!"

Charlotte gave a weak smile. "Well, that's a good start, then."

"We're going to miss you in the Final," Leela said.

"Just make sure you win," Charlotte said. "I don't want to go home with a losers' medal."

Leela nodded. "But Ashfield beat us 2–0 in the last round, and they won their semi-final pretty easy, too."

Leela was right. The all-boys' squad of Ashfield School was full of confidence.

They even ran onto the pitch in an arrow-shaped formation. Then they did some warm-up exercises.

"Huh! Just look at that load of dummies!" scoffed Harry. "Who do they think they're going to impress?"

"Us, probably," said Oliver, who was going to play up front. "Are you OK in that sweat shirt?"

Harry had borrowed Oliver's green sweatshirt. It was a bit small for him, but it was that or Charlotte's yellow jersey.

"Yeah, I'm fine," he lied. He didn't feel at all OK about playing in goal. "Just make sure you score more goals than I let in!"

They grinned at each other.

"Come on, get in goal and I'll take a few shots at you," Oliver told him.

They did not have long. Harry was soon called by the referee to toss up with the Ashfield captain.

"Heads!" called Harry as the coin spun into the air.

"Tails," said the referee.

That wasn't the only thing that Harry got wrong.

Ashfield swept into the attack straight from the kick-off. It took a well-timed tackle by Ravi, to prevent an early shot at goal.

Harry's first task as goalie was to block a low shot with his legs instead of his hands. He used his hands for his second task – picking the ball out of the net after the rebound had been smashed back past him.

"Unlucky, skipper," said Brad.

Harry booted the ball away in a temper.

"Huh! Any chance of *you* trying to stop them shooting?"

Brad and Ravi kept Ashfield at bay for the rest of the first period. Most of Ashfield's shots were long-distance efforts which caused Harry few problems, but their own keeper had nothing to do.

Then Gateway won a free kick for a foul on Leela. Oliver took it. The ball swerved and dipped as it flew, but the keeper got it away to one side.

Just before the interval, there was a goal that nobody expected.

Leela was boxed in against the side wall
of the pitch. She kicked the ball back to Brad
who had moved up in support of the attack,
crossing the halfway line for the first time in
the game.

Brad pushed the ball in front of him,
looking for a Gateway player to pass to, but
everyone was well marked.

So Brad went even further forward and ran out of options. The only thing he could do was shoot.

Ashfield realised the danger too late. Before anyone could try to block the shot, the ball was bouncing back out of the net.

"I've scored!" Brad screamed in disbelief. "Incredible!"

Chapter Seven

Golden Goals

"Take over from me," Harry told Ravi at half-time. "I want to get back out onto the pitch."

Ravi was about to argue when Mrs Phillips saw Harry taking off the green top.

"Just a minute, Harry," she said. "What are you doing?"

"Er… letting Ravi go in goal."

"Did I say anything about that?" she asked.

"Well, no, but…"

"So put it back on, please, Harry," she told him. "I don't want to make any changes yet. We've just drawn level and you're doing fine in goal."

"But…" Harry began.

"No *buts*, Harry, please. Just do as I say."

Harry was cross but he didn't argue. He had a sulky look as he tugged the sweatshirt back on.

"Well done, everyone," said Mrs Phillips, ignoring the captain's sighs. "We're back in this game now!"

Gateway started the second half with a goal.

Leela struck the ball perfectly with her left foot, curling it into the top corner to give Gateway a 2–1 lead.

"Magic!" cried Charlotte from the side.

Ashfield went on the attack, but good defending by Brad and Ravi, plus two more saves from Harry, stopped them from scoring.

It looked like Gateway were winning –
until they gave away the lead. Every single
Gateway player was at fault, ending up with a
howler by Harry.

Oliver gave the ball away too easily.
Leela's tackle was weak, Ravi fell over, and
the ball rolled through Brad's legs into the
path of Ashfield's top scorer.

The striker's shot was tame and Harry did
not bother to save it with his hands. He used
his feet, planning to kick the ball up to Oliver.

So when the ball bobbled over his foot,
Harry had no chance. He swiped at thin air
and the ball rolled slowly into the net behind
him.

The laughter around the arena did not
make Harry feel any better. He crouched
down, head in hands, unable to look anybody
in the eye.

Mrs Phillips took pity on the captain and decided to give him a chance to make up for his mistake.

"Go in goal now, Ravi," she called out. "Let Harry play up front for the last few minutes."

Harry ripped off the green top and ran across to the team base for his red shirt. Charlotte tossed it to him, making no comment about the mistake. She knew exactly how it felt to let in a soft goal.

"Go and grab the winner," she said.

Harry very nearly did so. In Gateway's
next attack, the ball dropped at his feet, but
he scooped his hurried shot over the low
crossbar.

There was still enough time for either
school to snatch a victory with a late goal, and
Ashfield nearly did. Their striker had a good
chance to pass the ball to a team-mate, but he
wanted a hat-trick, so he tried to score instead.

Ravi managed to get both hands to the ball and cling on to it.

"Rave-save!" Harry cried. "Better than I could have done."

When the referee blew for full-time, with the scores tied at 2–2, the Gateway players braced themselves for penalties again. But instead the referee said they would go into extra time.

"Two minutes each way," the referee called, "but if one team scores, that's the end of the game. It's the Golden Goal rule."

Harry liked the sound of that. "*Golden Goal*!" he cried. "That's what it's all about today. Every goal has been worth its weight in gold!"

Midway through the first period, Leela passed to Harry. He saw a chance to score.

He would be the hero if he got the winning goal! Harry drew his right foot back to shoot – but it was a tricky angle. He thought of the Ashfield striker's greedy miss.

So, Harry didn't try to score himself. Instead, he passed the ball to Oliver, who was in a better position.

Oliver hit the ball low and hard, and it skimmed into the back of the net.

"Hot-shot!" screamed Harry. "We've won!"

Oliver and Brad grabbed one of Harry's legs each, and he was given a bumpy ride around the pitch on Ravi's shoulders. Leela and Charlotte leapt around them like playful puppies.

"We got thirteen goals!" cried Leela.

"Lucky thirteen!" laughed Charlotte.

After Harry had lifted the County Cup to cheers, clapping and cameras, Mrs Phillips had some good news.

"The school will double the sponsor money," she told them, "so Saint Francis will receive over a thousand pounds. That will buy them a lot of footballs!"

The youngsters whooped their delight and then ran off with the trophy and their medals to do another lap of honour.

"Talk about Golden Goals!" laughed Harry.